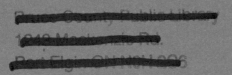

Stories at the Door

By Jan Andrews
Illustrations by Francis Blake

Tundra Books

Text copyright © 2007 by Jan Andrews
Illustrations copyright © 2007 by Francis Blake

Published in Canada by Tundra Books,
75 Sherbourne Street, Toronto, Ontario M5A 2P9

Published in the United States by Tundra Books of Northern New York,
P.O. Box 1030, Plattsburgh, New York 12901

Library of Congress Control Number: 2006909136

Library and Archives Canada Cataloguing in Publication

Andrews, Jan, 1942-
        Stories at the door / Jan Andrews ; illustrated by Francis Blake.

ISBN 978-0-88776-811-8

        1. Tales—Juvenile fiction.   I. Blake, Francis   II. Title.

PS8551.N37S76 2007   jC813'.54   C2006-905783-4

We acknowledge the financial support of the Government of Canada through
the Book Publishing Industry Development Program (BPIDP) and that of
the Government of Ontario through the Ontario Media Development Corporation's
Ontario Book Initiative. We further acknowledge the support of the Canada Council
for the Arts and the Ontario Arts Council for our publishing program.

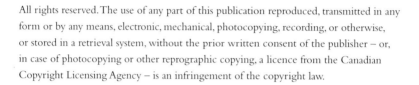

ONTARIO ARTS COUNCIL
CONSEIL DES ARTS DE L'ONTARIO

Design: Terri Nimmo

Printed and bound in China

1 2 3 4 5 6   12 11 10 09 08 07

To Marie, for leaps of faith
J.A.

For Lilly and for Louise
F.B.

What's that at the door?

It's a story! A story by gosh and by gum.

I can see from its nose and its whiskers.

I can see from its tail and its tum.

It stopped on the step for a moment.

It dithered a while on the mat.

But now it's come in. It's about to begin.

It's even hung up its own hat.

ONE

JESPER AND THE JACKRABBITS

Once upon a time – that wasn't your time or my time – there was a lumber baron. There was also a lad named Jesper. The lumber baron lived in a fancy, great house in a town by a river. He'd made his money out of other men's work at the logging. He was big and fat and rich.

Jesper lived with his mother and his father and his two older brothers on a little wee farm where the soil was mean and rocky. He was like all the rest of the family. He was small and thin and poor.

The lumber baron had a daughter. He wanted to find a husband for her, so he sent word to all his friends and neighbors – and rich folks far away even – saying that any man who wanted to make her his bride should come.

When that man came, he should bring something rare with him. If that thing was rare enough, he'd be allowed to try certain tests.

There was many a man arrived. The lumber baron soon had more rare things than he knew what to do with. Rare birds, rare beasts; rare cloth and clothes and carriages; rare tables and rare chairs; rare pots and plates and ornaments; rare unmentionables. Unfortunately, none of the suitors for his daughter's hand had any brains in their heads. The baron's tests got easier and easier, but there wasn't a one of the suitors could succeed at even the simplest task.

Word of the contest spread. Poor as they were, even Jesper's family got to hear about it.

"Wouldn't that be fine then – to marry the lumber baron's daughter?" the oldest brother said.

"We don't have something rare to take to him," the middle brother answered.

Jesper didn't say anything. He often didn't when his older brothers were around.

Here's what's strange, though. Just that very day their father was plowing a new piece of land. The plow was going along and going along and then it got stuck. The father thought the blade had caught on a bit of leftover root, but it hadn't. The blade had caught on an ancient, buried chest. The father brought the brothers to help him dig the chest out.

Here's what's stranger. When they opened the lid, they found that inside there were golden coins and diamonds. There was also a round, metal object with a date set on it. The date was 1603.

The father was pleased enough, because now his sons could have their chance. He told the brothers to choose what they wanted. The oldest brother chose the gold coins. The middle brother chose the diamonds. Jesper had to take the round metal object with the date on it. What did his brothers care about that?

The oldest brother put his gold coins in a basket. He covered the basket with a cloth. Early next morning, he set off. He walked a ways and walked a ways. In the road he came upon a column of ants. They were bringing food back to their nest, but they had to go down into this hollow and up the other side again to get there. The hollow made a longer journey.

"Would you smooth the road out for us?" the king of the ants called up to him.

"I'm in too much of a hurry. I'm going to marry the lumber baron's daughter," the oldest brother answered.

He hardly even stopped to catch his breath.

When it was getting to be almost lunchtime, he came upon an old woman sitting beside the road.

"What are you carrying?" she asked him.

He reckoned he was much too smart to tell her he had gold coins with him. "Ashes," he answered.

The old woman gave a smile and a wave to him. "Ashes it be," she said.

On he went again. He came to the town. He got directions to the lumber baron's house; he knocked on the door.

"What have you brought me?" the lumber baron asked him.

"Gold coins," the oldest brother said.

He lifted the cloth. The gold coins were there all right; they were gleaming. But they turned to ashes before the lumber baron's eyes. The ashes were gray and cold and dusty. They got up the lumber baron's nose.

The oldest brother was sent home. He didn't tell about what had happened and the middle brother didn't ask.

"Diamonds are better than gold, for certain," the middle brother said.

He took that same basket. He put his diamonds into it. He covered it with a cloth.

Oh, he was excited. So excited, he didn't even notice the ants till he was almost treading on them.

"Would you smooth the road out for us?" the king of the ants called up to him.

The middle brother didn't even bother to answer. When it was just about lunchtime, he came to the old woman. She was still there, sitting beside the road.

"What is it you're carrying?" she asked him.

9

Would I be such a fool as to tell her? he thought to himself. "Ducklings," he answered.

"Ducklings it be," she said.

Ducklings it was, too. The lumber baron had just long enough to catch a glimpse of the diamonds and be all thrilled about them, before the diamonds turned to ducklings in front of his very eyes. The ducklings went cheeping and scrambling out of the basket; they waddled into all sorts of places where they weren't supposed to go.

That was it for the middle brother too, then.

Jesper had been polishing up the metal object and oiling it while his two older brothers had been off on their adventures. He'd discovered the arrow part that went across it could move.

The next morning, he dressed himself in his cleanest, least-old shirt. He put on his Sunday suit that was handed down to him when his middle brother had grown out of it. He put on his Sunday boots that didn't have so many holes. He set the metal object in the basket. He covered the basket with a cloth.

His brothers didn't even notice him going. Still, he set out laughing and singing a tune. He walked a ways and walked a ways. He came to where the ants were working to get their food home.

"Will you smooth the road out for us?" the king of the ants called up to him.

"Of course, I will," he said.

He waited for all the ants to climb up safely out of the hollow. He smoothed the road until it was flat.

"That was a great kindness," the king of the ants said to him. "If you should need us, you have only to think of us and we will come."

"I'll remember that," said Jesper.

Off he went again, laughing and singing some more. He came to the old woman.

"What is it you're carrying?" she asked him.

"It's something rare," he told her.

"Will you show it to me?" she asked him.

"Of course, I will," he said, and he got the metal object out.

"That is rare," the old woman said, when she'd finished looking at it.

"Do you know what it is?" Jesper asked her.

She looked again – more carefully. She held the object up. She moved the arrow part about. "I'd say it's what a long-ago explorer might have used to find his way," she answered finally. "Maybe that famous Samuel de Champlain fellow even."

"I'll remember that," said Jesper.

"Do you have any lunch with you?" the old woman asked him.

"I have some bread," he told her.

"Will you share it with me?" the old woman asked him.

"Of course, I will," said Jesper.

Jesper took out the bread and broke it. He gave the old woman the biggest piece.

"Here's something for you," she said, when they'd finished eating. "It's a whistle, but there's a magic to it. One blow on it and whatever you've lost will come back."

"I'll remember that," said Jesper.

He thanked the old woman very much. Off he went again, still laughing and singing. It was evening, almost, before he came to the lumber baron's great, big door and got shown into the lumber baron's great, big house.

"What have your brought me?" the lumber baron asked him.

"Something old," said Jesper, pointing out the date. "Something rare."

The lumber baron couldn't deny that.

"You'll have to say what it's for," the lumber baron insisted.

Jesper held the object up. He moved the arrow part. "A long-ago explorer found his way with it. Maybe the famous Samuel de Champlain even," he answered.

The lumber baron looked Jesper over more closely. He saw his least-old shirt and his handed-down suit and his boots with the not-so-many holes in.

The lumber baron waited. He was hoping the old, rare object would turn into something else. The old, rare object sat there in the basket.

"You'll have to take the tests. The first one's in the morning," the lumber baron said.

The lumber baron went to bed to rack his brains.

When Jesper came back – in the morning – he was met by one of the lumber baron's servants. The servant took him to a lumber mill. The servant showed him a pile of sawdust, higher than his head.

"There's all kinds of wood in there. There's dust from pine and spruce and maple and birch and oak, and you're to sort it. And you're to have it done by evening," the servant said.

Jesper scratched his head, but not for very long.

He thought about the ants. They came, just like they'd promised. By the time the servant got back in the evening, there was a heap of pine sawdust and a heap of spruce sawdust; a heap of maple sawdust and a heap of birch sawdust; a heap of oak sawdust and a heap of basswood sawdust that the servant hadn't even spoken of. Jesper was stretched out having a nap.

The lumber baron told Jesper to come back the next day. The lumber baron went to bed to rack his brains again.

This time when the servant came, he took Jesper to a field. In the field there were one hundred cages. In each of the cages there was a jackrabbit.

"You're to guard the jackrabbits all day and not lose even a one of them," the servant said.

The servant went from one cage to another. He let the jackrabbits out. Off they went, the whole lot of them, their tails bobbing; a hundred jackrabbits in a hundred different directions. Soon enough, there wasn't a jackrabbit to be seen.

Jesper scratched his head, but not for very long.

He waited until the servant was out of sight. He took the old woman's whistle from his pocket. He gave a little, small tweet on it. The jackrabbits all came bounding back.

"You're to stay in the field," he told them. "You can nibble the grass to your hearts' content, but you're not to leave."

A couple of hours later, when the servant arrived to see how things were going, there was Jesper sitting in the sun. The jackrabbits were nibbling away all round him. The servant couldn't believe his eyes. He went and told the lumber baron. The lumber baron told his daughter and his wife.

Not so very long after that a girl came to the field, all dressed in rags.

"I've nothing to eat for my supper and no money," she said to Jesper. "Will you give me one of your jackrabbits to cook?"

Jesper looked her up and he looked her down and he thought a little. By then, the girl in rags was crying.

"Of course, I'll give you one of my jackrabbits," he answered. "I'll give you one of my jackrabbits, if you'll give me a kiss on the cheek."

The girl in rags wasn't too pleased. She kissed him on the cheek anyway. She kissed him where he showed her. Jesper caught one of the jackrabbits and gave it to her. She started to carry it off. As soon as she stepped from the field, he blew the whistle. A kick and a squirm. The jackrabbit was out of the girl's arms and at Jesper's feet once more, before she could barely blink.

Jesper sat down in the sun again. In half an hour or so, a woman came walking to the field. She was even more poorly dressed than the girl had been.

"It's terrible," she said. "I've nothing to feed my children. Would you give me just one of your jackrabbits to make a stew with?"

Jesper looked her up and he looked her down and he thought
a little.

She was crying also. She was crying very loudly, indeed.

"Of course, I'll give you one of my jackrabbits," he said to her.
"But it's a long day, sitting here watching. I'm in need of some
entertainment. I'll give you one of my jackrabbits if you'll go
round and round me, flapping your arms and squatting down here
and there and clucking like a hen."

"I can't do that," said the woman.

"I'm sorry then," said Jesper.

"Since it's for my children . . ." said the woman.

Off she went, flapping her arms and squatting about and
clucking. Three times round, like Jesper told her. He caught one of
the jackrabbits. He gave it to her. She started to carry it off. No
sooner had she stepped from the field, than he blew his whistle. A
flick of its nose and a wiggle. The jackrabbit was at his feet.

Hardly any time after that, Jesper saw a man approaching. The
man was wearing a jerkin, like a servant's.

"It's on my master's behalf I've come," the man said. "My
master wants a jackrabbit for his dinner. If I don't get it for him, I'll
lose my position. I'm only asking for one."

Jesper looked the man up and he looked him down and he
thought a little. The man was shaking. He was rubbing his hands
together in fear.

"Of course, I'll give you one of my jackrabbits," said Jesper.
"But I'm still in need of entertainment. I'll give you one of my

jackrabbits, if you'll stand on your head and kick your heels together and call out 'Hurrah.'"

"I can't do that," said the man.

"I'll help you," said Jesper.

He did, too. He had the man standing on his head and kicking his heels together and shouting out "Hurrah," in two seconds flat.

The man got his jackrabbit. The man set one foot outside the field. Jesper blew on his whistle. A twitch of its ears and a shiggle. The jackrabbit was at Jesper's feet.

That was it. Nothing else happened. The day came to an end. The jackrabbits were counted. There wasn't a one that was missing.

The lumber baron was desperate. So were his daughter and his wife. The lumber baron told Jesper to come back the next day. The lumber baron went to bed to rack his brains once more. All night, he worried and worried but, by the morning, he had an idea.

When Jesper arrived there were a lot a people gathered. The lumber baron had summoned all of his friends and his neighbors to be witnesses. In the middle of the room, there was a barrel — a cask such as might be used for keeping wine or salt meat.

"You're to set this barrel brimming with complete and utter truths," the lumber baron said.

"How will I know when it's full?" asked Jesper.

"I'll know and I'll tell you," the lumber baron answered.

A little laugh went round.

Jesper scratched his head, but not for very long.

"Here's what we'll start with," he said. "It has to do with yesterday when I was minding the jackrabbits. A girl came to me. She was pretty, but she was dressed in rags and she was poor. She said she was hungry. She wanted me to give her a jackrabbit to cook for her supper. I told her I would, but there was one condition. She must give me a kiss, right here, on my cheek. I thought she wouldn't, but she did."

"You can't prove that," said the lumber baron.

"I can," said Jesper. "For I can see the girl right here."

"Which one is she?" said the lumber baron.

"It's your daughter," said Jesper.

The baron's daughter blushed from her chin to the roots of her hair. A bigger laugh swelled up.

The lumber baron peered into the barrel. "It's still almost empty," he declared.

"Well," said Jesper, "Here's another thing. It was a very busy day there, with the jackrabbits. Your daughter had hardly gone when a woman came after her. She was in rags as well – only her rags were worse. She said she had nothing to feed her children. She wanted me to give her a jackrabbit. I told her I couldn't unless she would go round me three times flapping her arms and squatting down here and there and clucking like a hen. I thought she wouldn't, but she did."

"You can't prove that," said the lumber baron.

"I can," said Jesper. "For I can see the woman right here."

"Which one is she?" said the lumber baron.

"It's your wife," said Jesper.

By then, the face of the lumber baron's wife was even redder than her daughter's. It looked like fire had come to it. The laughter swelled up louder. People were clutching their sides.

The lumber baron didn't just peer into the barrel. He felt about in it.

"Not even the bottom is covered yet," the lumber baron said.

"Try this then," said Jesper. "It might take up more room. After your wife was gone, a man came. He was wearing a jerkin, like a servant's. He told me he needed a jackrabbit for his master to put in a pie, or something. He said if I didn't give him one, he'd lose his job. I didn't want him to get into trouble. Of course I didn't. I told him I'd give him a jackrabbit if he'd stand on his head and kick his heels together and call out 'Hurrah.' I thought he wouldn't, but he did."

"You can't prove that," said the lumber baron.

"I can," said Jesper. "For I can see the man right here."

"The barrel is full! The barrel is full!" shouted the lumber baron.

"Can I marry your daughter then?" Jesper asked him.

"I'll pay for the wedding," the lumber baron said.

Jesper scratched his head, but not for very long.

"I don't think we should marry until we've had time to find out if we like each other," he announced.

The lumber baron's daughter couldn't believe her ears. She was so pleased, she kissed Jesper on the cheek again. She did it twice for all the world to see.

Turned out she was more than willing to take all the time that was needed. Both of them were, in fact. That's how they came to love each other. That's how they came to live together happy as may be, and happy as might.

What's that at the door?
It's a story! A story by golly, by gee.
I can tell from its long dangly earlobes,
And from how it's sat down on my knee.

It's taken a turn round the kitchen.
It's nibbled on cookies and cake.
I'm certain that now it is ready.
It's starting to tremble and shake.

JACINTHE WINS WORDS

Y ou can believe this or not, as you've a fancy. But it's as
true as the nose on your face.

Once upon a time – that wasn't your time or my
time – there were two sisters. The older one was a bit of a meanie.
She scratched and scraped for every cent and penny. Jacinthe, she
was the younger one, and she was very generous. She shared whatever she had.

The two sisters worked in a part of town where there was a
market. They both had different jobs. The older sister, her job was in
a store. The store sold fruits and flowers and vegetables. She'd done
very well for herself. She was the manager – the one in charge.

Jacinthe wasn't so lucky. Her job was outside, at a stall. The stall
had scarves and beads and funny little toys that didn't bring in
much money. In the summer, the sun beat down on it so Jacinthe
would be sweating and burning, even under her great, big, straw
sun hat; in the winter the cold would make it so her toes and
fingers ached and tingled. She always had to be swinging her arms
about and stamping her feet.

The two sisters didn't live together. They had their own apartments, although the older sister's was much finer. Jacinthe lived in a basement where the windows weren't big enough and she had to keep folding her bed up to make space.

Mostly, the hours Jacinthe worked were very long, but on this one day, she got off early. She thought how she hadn't seen her older sister for ages. She decided she'd go and find out how she was. There were a lot of people about. There always were in the market. Jacinthe had to push her way through the crowds, but she didn't mind that. She greeted the ones who knew her. She even helped some of them carry their groceries and choose their bread and meat and fish.

At last, she came to where her sister's store was. As she walked through the door, she saw a pile of red, red pomegranates – the very first pomegranates of the season. They were heaped up in a pyramid.

Jacinthe went toward them. She picked one up. She touched it to her cheek. She checked in her change purse. She saw she hardly had enough money to buy her supper. She put the pomegranate back.

Her sister was watching all of this. She could have taken a pomegranate to the cash and paid for it and given it to Jacinthe and never known the difference.

Instead, she thought to herself, *Is it my fault if my younger sister has so little money?* Then she thought, *What does she need with pomegranates anyway?* Then: *If I bought her one, I know what she'd do with it. She'd give it away.*

That was it for Jacinthe's pomegranate.

The two sisters visited together for a while and Jacinthe went home. But she couldn't forget about those fruits. She just couldn't. She knew they'd be so sweet and juicy on her tongue.

The next day was payday. As soon as she'd got her wages, she went to her sister's store. She chose the pomegranate that looked best to her. She put her money down. She didn't even wait to get home. She cut the pomegranate in half with a little knife she kept in her pocket. She went walking through the market, sucking the pomegranate pulp and keeping the pomegranate seeds in her hand to put in the garbage later, like the careful person that she was.

The pomegranate tasted even better than she'd expected. The first half was just about gone when she saw a young man walking toward her. He came to the market often. She'd been watching him and wanting to talk properly to him for a long, long while. And now, she had something to give him.

"Would you like a piece of my pomegranate?" she asked him, once they'd said their hellos.

"I would," the young man answered.

Jacinthe cut the second half of the pomegranate into two pieces. She and the young man kept walking. Only now they were together, both of them sucking the pomegranate pulp and keeping the seeds safe in their hands. Jacinthe thought maybe the young man was beginning to enjoy her company. She was certainly enjoying his. He was like the man of her dreams – the handsomest thing in all the world to her. He asked her if she'd like to go and have a cup of coffee with him.

"Oh, yes, I would," she said.

Into the restaurant they went; down they sat. The coffee came. They were having a lovely time, the two of them, when the worst thing ever happened. Jacinthe felt a rumbling in her tummy. She let out this great big fart.

She was sure it was the end of everything between them.

Why can't the earth just swallow me up? she thought.

The earth did. Before she knew it, she was in another market-place. It was very much like the one she'd come from. Everything was bright and fair. There were people jostling and shoving and

calling out to one another and laughing at this, that, and the other thing, just the same way.

She was so upset about the fart she decided she'd look for it.

"Have you seen a fart?" she started asking passersby.

"Why would you search for a fart?" someone demanded.

Jacinthe explained about how she'd been embarrassed.

"The fart must be punished! The fart must be punished!" the people round her cried.

Soon there was a whole great crowd of them; they were charging about in all directions. They were all of them yelling and shouting: "Find the fart! Find the fart! Find the fart!"

Finally, a cry went up that was louder than any of the others. "We have him! We have him! He's here!"

The fart *was* there, too. He was a big, strong fellow. He was dressed in a fine, new set of clothing, with a tie and a jacket. He was sitting on a bench and enjoying himself, eating a piece of blueberry pie.

The crowd pushed Jacinthe forward. "Shame on you for harming her!" the people raged.

"What did I do?" the fart demanded.

"You escaped! You came out against her will! You embarrassed her!"

"But I was so crushed and uncomfortable. If I'd stayed where I was a minute longer, I'd have suffocated."

"That is only an excuse!"

"Can you not see that I made the right decision? Do you not know that I am better off out here?"

The members of the crowd weren't satisfied. All in a group, they went looking for the mayor. The mayor was brought back, wearing his chain of office.

"You must do something for this young woman to make amends," he decreed.

"I shall see to it that whenever she speaks, her words bring rewards to her," the fart said.

The mayor asked Jacinthe if this would be sufficient. Jacinthe said that it would. The mayor and the crowd were pleased. Jacinthe thanked the fart and the mayor and everyone else who had helped her.

"But how am I to get home again?" she asked.

"That's not difficult," said the fart. "All you have to do is say 'Let the earth bring me up.'"

Jacinthe decided she'd try it. "Let the earth bring me up," she said.

As she spoke, she felt her lips grow warmer. It was a good feeling. She was really too busy to notice much, however, for quick as a wink, she was back in the restaurant. Hardly any time had passed, in fact. The young man was still there. He thought she'd just gone to the washroom. He smiled his lovely smile at her. They drank their coffee. They decided they should meet again.

Jacinthe was so delighted, she didn't give the fart's promise another thought – not till the next day. Then, she found that people were buying twice as much as they ever did from her. They were happier about it, too. She told her boss; he gave her a raise without her even asking. She saw she'd been given a gift.

She could hardly wait to tell her sister all about it. On her way home she went to her sister's store.

"You'll never guess what happened!" she burst out.

Her sister listened. She wasn't the only one, though. Everyone else stopped what they were doing so they wouldn't miss anything Jacinthe was saying. All of them clapped and cheered when she was done. An important man was among the shoppers.

"I'll make you famous," he said.

The older sister was angry. *If all I have to do to become famous is to fart and be embarrassed, then tomorrow I shall fart as well*, she thought.

The trouble was, she couldn't get a fart out of herself. Not one. She tried when she was taking orders from the store's owner; she tried when she was helping the store's richest customer. She tried when she was in a meeting telling everyone else who worked with her what to do. She was about to give up, when the richest man in the city entered.

This is the moment, the older sister thought.

She huffed and she puffed; she squeezed till her face was purple with the effort. At last, she managed it. It was only a short squeak. She didn't know whether the rich man had heard, or whether he hadn't. She wasn't going to wait to find out.

"May the earth swallow me up," she said.

The earth did. She, too, was in a marketplace, except this one was very cold and very dark. Rain was falling. Everything was poor and wretched. Everyone looked as if what they wanted most of all in all the world was to be somewhere else.

The older sister didn't care about that.

"Have you seen a fart?" she demanded of the people passing by.

Before they even asked, she told them how she'd been embarrassed.

There weren't that many of them. Still, "The fart must be punished! The fart must be punished!" they agreed.

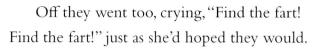

Off they went too, crying, "Find the fart! Find the fart!" just as she'd hoped they would. They searched until the shout came. "We have him! We have him! He's here."

They brought her to where the fart was. They pushed her forward.

The fart was so weak and thin, he was huddled in a corner. His rags hardly covered him. He was shivering. His hair was sodden from the rain.

"What do you want with me?" he asked.

"You embarrassed this woman."

"Do you think I wanted to?"

"How should we know?"

"Why should I want to when I was warm and happy inside her? When I would have stayed there forever if she hadn't worked and worked to force me out?"

The members of the crowd didn't know what to do. They went to find the mayor. The mayor was a little puzzled but at last he decided, "You must give this woman something for her trouble."

"I will make it so that, whenever she speaks, her words will be like wasp stings," the fart said.

"Let the earth take me up," the older sister cried quickly. Even as she did so, she felt a fiery stabbing on her lips.

That's how it was from then on, always. Her words brought pain to her; they brought pain to everyone else as well.

As for Jacinthe, she liked being famous. She also liked having more money, but she didn't let it change her. She went on being kind and she went on sharing; she went on coming to the market-place and meeting people. Why wouldn't she? For her, the best reward was cheering people up.

She and the young man got to be the best of friends but they never did marry. Why they didn't is really their own business, so most like we shouldn't even try to find out.

Whats that at the door?

It's a story. I can tell that at once – by a glance.

I can see from its long curly toenails,

And from how it's beginning to dance.

I think we should give it a welcome.

I think we should make it some tea.

I think we should say we'll be listening.

We're not heading off up a tree.

A CAT AND MOUSE TALE

Once upon a time – that wasn't your time or my time – but was long enough ago that folks were still spinning their wool into yarn in their own homes; once upon a time, if you're ready to imagine it, there was a cat.

She had this spinning wheel and she was always using it. She'd sit by the stove with it. She'd spin and spin. She'd set the wheel whirring and thrumming so the whole house was filled up with the noise.

There was a little, wee mouse that lived in a hole in the wall, and he was being driven crazy by the sound. He ran out and he bit off the cat's thread. The cat had to stop her work, even if it was only for a minute.

"If you do that again, I'll bite your tail off," she said.

The very next day, as soon as the cat started spinning, the mouse got this terrible headache. Out he ran.

"I warned you, didn't I?" the cat said.

The mouse bit her thread off anyway. He couldn't help himself.

Just as the cat had promised, she bit off his tail. All he had left was this little, small stump of a thing.

"Oh, please," said the mouse. "Give me my nice, long tail back. I need it to wrap around me when I'm sleeping in the winter that is so icy and so cold."

"I will give you back your tail," said the cat, "but you must do something for me. You must go to the cow and bring me a saucer of milk."

"I will! I will!" said the mouse.

He went to the cow as quick as he could run there.

"Cow," he said, "I must have a saucer of milk to take to the cat, so she'll give me my nice, long tail back that I need to wrap around me when I'm sleeping in the winter that is so icy and so cold."

"I will give you a saucer of milk," said the cow, "but you must do something for me. You must go to the barn and bring me a bale of hay."

"I will! I will!" said the mouse.

He went to the barn as quick as he could run there.

"Barn," he said, "I must have a bale of hay to take to the cow, so she'll give me a saucer of milk to take to the cat, so she'll give me my nice, long tail back that I need to wrap around me when I'm sleeping in the winter that is so icy and so cold."

"I will give you a bale of hay," said the barn, "but you must do something for me. You must go to the locksmith and bring me a key for my lock."

"I will! I will!" said the mouse.

He went to the locksmith as quick as he could run there.

"Locksmith," he said, "I must have a key to take to the barn, so the barn will give me a bale of hay to take to the cow, so the cow will give me a saucer of milk to take to the cat, so the cat will give me my nice, long tail back that I need to wrap around me when I'm sleeping in the winter that is so icy and so cold."

"I will give you a key," said the locksmith, "but you must do something for me. You must go to the mine and bring me a sack of coal."

"I will! I will!" said the mouse.

He went to the mine as quick as he could run there.

"Mine," he said, "I must have a sack of coal to take to the locksmith, so the locksmith will give me a key to take to the barn, so the barn will give me a bale of hay to take to the cow, so the cow will give me a saucer of milk to take to the cat, so the cat will give me my nice, long tail back that I need to wrap around me when I'm sleeping in the winter that is so icy and so cold."

"I will give you a sack of coal," said the mine, "but you must do something for me. You must go to the raven and bring me one of his feathers."

"I will! I will!" said the mouse.

He went to the raven as quick as he could run there.

"Raven," he said, "I must have one of your feathers to take to the mine, so the mine will give me a sack of coal to take to the locksmith, so the locksmith will give me a key to take to the barn, so the barn will give me a bale of hay to take to the cow, so the cow will give me a saucer of milk to take to the cat, so the cat will give me my nice, long tail back that I need to wrap around me when I'm sleeping in the winter that is so icy and so cold."

"I will give you one of my feathers," said the raven, "but you must do something for me. You must go to the sow and bring me one of her piglets."

"I will! I will!" said the mouse.

He went to the sow as quick as he could run there.

"Sow," he said, "I must have one of your piglets to take to the raven, so the raven will give me one of his feathers to take to the mine, so the mine will give me a sack of coal to take to the locksmith, so the lock-smith will give me a key to take to the barn, so the barn will give me a bale of hay to take to the cow, so the cow will give me a saucer of milk to take to the cat, so the cat will give me my nice, long tail back that I need to wrap around me when I'm sleeping in the winter that is so icy and so cold."

"I will give you one of my piglets," said the sow, "but you must do something for me. You must go to the cheese maker and fetch me a bucket of swill."

"I will! I will!" said the mouse.

He went to the cheese maker as quick as he could run there.

"Cheese maker," he said, "I must have a bucket of swill to take to the sow, so she will give me one of her piglets to take to the raven, so the raven will give me one of his feathers to take to the mine, so the mine will give me a sack of coal to take to the locksmith, so the locksmith will give me a key to take to the barn, so the barn will give me a bale of hay to take to the cow, so the cow will give me a saucer of milk to take to the cat, so the cat will give me my nice, long tail back that I need to wrap around me when I'm sleeping in the winter that is so icy and so cold."

"I will give you a bucket of swill," said the cheese maker, "but you must do something for me. You must go to the well to fetch me a bucket of water."

"I will! I will!" said the mouse.

He came to the well as quick as he could run there.

"Well," he said, "I must have a bucket of water to take to the cheese maker, so he will give me a bucket of swill to take to the sow, so the sow will give me one of her piglets to take to the raven, so the raven will give me one of his feathers to take to the mine, so the mine will give me a sack of coal to take to the locksmith, so the locksmith will give me a key to take to the barn, so the barn will give me a bale of hay to take to the cow, so the cow will give me a saucer of milk to take to the cat, so the cat will give me my nice, long tail back that I need to wrap around me when I'm sleeping in the winter that is so icy and so cold."

"I will give you a bucket of water," said the well, "but you will have to haul it up."

MILK

THE MINE

COAL

CHEESE MAKER

SWILL

"I will! I will!" said the mouse.

He hauled up the bucket of water. He took the bucket of water to the cheese maker. The cheese maker gave the mouse a bucket of swill. The mouse took the bucket of swill to the sow. The sow gave the mouse one of her piglets. The mouse took the piglet to the raven. The raven gave the mouse one of his feathers. The mouse took the feather to the mine. The mine gave the mouse a sack of coal. The mouse took the sack of coal to the locksmith. The locksmith gave the mouse a key. The mouse took the key to the barn. The barn gave the mouse a bale of hay. The mouse took the hay to the cow. The cow gave the mouse a saucer of milk. The mouse took the milk to the cat.

"What a long time you've taken," the cat said.

She lapped up the milk and she gave the mouse his tail back.

He didn't just wrap it around him when he was sleeping in the winter that is so icy and so cold. He wrapped it around him when the cat set the spinning wheel to whirring and to thrumming. He covered his ears with it. That way, he never got another headache. He wasn't tempted to bite the cat's thread off ever again for the rest of his life.

And if you're wanting to know why the mine needed a feather, I'll tell you. It's because a feather is so light. If a feather was on the floor of a mine, and that feather started to shake you'd know the earth was moving and the walls were about to come tumbling. Isn't that interesting, then?

What's that at the door?
It's a story. It's entering in with a bow.
It's come in a sort of a carriage,
Though really I'm not quite sure how.

It seems to be awfully eager.
It's finding a place on a chair.
It's telling us all to come closer.
It just wants us all to be there.

JAMILLA FINDS FEAR

O nce upon a time – that wasn't my time or your time, but it certainly was a long-ago time – there was a girl, and her name was Jamilla. She lived with her mother. They had a little store where people could get the things they needed. The store was in a village. The village was in a valley with forests all about.

One evening a wind came sighing through the village from the treetops. The sound of the wind was like a sad voice calling round the house.

"Close the doors and pull the drapes tighter together so I won't hear it. It makes me shudder," Jamilla's mother said.

"What is this shuddering?" Jamilla asked her.

"It's a shaking you get when you're afraid of something," her mother replied.

"I've never been afraid of anything," said Jamilla. "I've never shuddered."

"That worries me," her mother told her.

"Do you suppose, if I went looking in the world, I could find out how to shudder?" Jamilla demanded.

"I'm sure you could," her mother said.

First thing in the morning, Jamilla set off. She decided she'd start by talking to the schoolteacher. After all, he was the one who was supposed to know whatever needed knowing, because he read so many books.

The schoolteacher was in the schoolhouse.

"I have to learn to shudder," she told him.

"That shouldn't be so difficult," he said.

He caught a spider with great, long, hairy legs. He put the spider on the table. The spider ran toward Jamilla. She picked the spider up. She put it where no one would step on it.

"You're going to need more help than I can give you," the schoolteacher announced.

Jamilla thanked the schoolteacher for his trouble. She left the village and started to walk. She followed the road through the forest. She followed the road up hills and down into valleys. She followed it to where she saw a cabin off in the distance on the edge of a marsh. She knocked on the door, as bold as brass.

The cabin had thieves in it. The thieves had knives and swords.

"I have to learn to shudder," Jamilla told them.

The thieves were surprised she wasn't shuddering at them. They gave her a meal. They made their minds up they'd do whatever they could to help her.

"You stay with us through the day tomorrow," they said to her. "When it's nighttime, you get on the road again. You keep on walking. You'll come to a town. In the middle of the town you'll find a gallows. On the gallows you'll see the corpses of seven dead men. If you sit down beneath those corpses, you'll be set to shuddering for sure."

Jamilla thanked the thieves. She did as they'd told her. She waited through the daytime. At nighttime, she set off. She came to the town. She came to the gallows. She saw the seven dead corpses swinging and swaying from it. She sat herself down.

"We're longing for a bit of living company," the corpses moaned out to her.

"I'll be company for you," Jamilla said.

"You're so far away," the corpses cried.

"Come and sit with me then."

The corpses climbed down. They sat right beside her. They told her their troubles. They waited till the cock crowed to show that it was almost morning. They said good-bye to her and then they climbed back up.

So what was supposed to make me shudder? Jamilla wondered. *I'll go to those thieves and ask.*

The thieves were so surprised to see her, they ran off. They didn't even bother to take their weapons with them. Jamilla was more puzzled than ever. She kept on traveling.

"I have to learn to shudder," she said to everyone she came across along the way.

There were plenty that were ready to help her. Folks jumped out at her from behind trees and rocks and buildings; they led her into dark and dismal caves.

Someone sent her to a graveyard where a hand reached up out of the earth to grab her. She took hold of the hand and shook it. Someone else showed her how to find a huge, great monster. She sat the monster down and had a chat.

At last she came to where there was a river flowing down between two hillsides into the sea. On a hill by the river and over-looking the sea, there stood a mansion.

"That mansion's haunted. You'll shudder there," the folks living nearby told her.

Jamilla went to the mansion's owner. She got the key. She entered in through the mansion's gates at sunset. She put the key into the lock. The mansion was dirty and dusty, because no one had been in it for ages. Jamilla thought it could do with a cleanup, but she didn't mind.

Jamilla found a candle in a drawer in the kitchen. She lit the candle to give herself some light. She carried the candle into the enormous living room. She touched a match to the sticks and logs and paper that were ready in the fireplace. She settled herself in the rocking chair by the fire.

There was a clock in the living room. It struck one hour, and then it struck another. At ten o'clock, Jamilla heard a scratching.

"That must be someone wanting to come in," she said to herself.

She went to the door. She saw two cats as big as tigers, almost. The cats were spitting and hissing. The cats had eyes of flame and long, sharp claws. The cats had teeth with bloodstains.

"Are you the Cats of Hell?" Jamilla asked them.

"We are," the cats yeowled out.

"I expect you're wanting to warm yourselves," Jamilla said.

She brought the cats in. She let them sit by the fire. She stroked and stroked them. When the cats fell asleep, she fell asleep beside them. When she woke up in the morning, they were gone.

"I thought your mansion was where I was going to find out how to shudder," Jamilla said to the mansion's owner when she saw him.

"It's terrified everyone else who ever tried to sleep there so much, they've run out half dead with fright," the mansion's owner said. "Here's what we'll do, though. The mansion has a spell on it. If you can stay for two more nights, the spell will be broken. I'll give you a whole lot of money to take with you as a reward."

"Maybe tonight's the night there'll be something to make me shudder," Jamilla decided.

Back to the mansion she went; in through the gates at sunset.
She found herself another candle. She went into the living room.
She lit the fire. She settled herself in the rocking chair. The clock
struck one hour. It struck two more. When it struck eleven, she
heard a rattling and a dragging start up in the room above her.

"I suppose I should see what that is," she said to herself.

She took the candle and she went up the great, wide stairs. She
went into the room where the noise was. She saw a skeleton.

"Can I help you?" Jamilla asked it.

"I want to play catch, but I've no one to play with me," the
skeleton answered.

"I'll play with you. Of course, I will," Jamilla said.

The skeleton reached up.
It took its skull off. It tossed
the skull to her. Jamilla tossed
it back. They played for
maybe half an hour or more.

"I have to go to bed now,"
the skeleton said. "I'm tired."

"I'm tired too," said
Jamilla.

She went back down. She fell asleep in the rocking chair. In
the morning, she went upstairs and into that same room again. She
found the skeleton in a closet. It didn't speak to her, so she left it
where it was.

"I thought your mansion was where I was going to find out how
to shudder," Jamilla said to the mansion's owner when she saw him.

"There's only one more night till the spell is broken," the mansion's owner answered. "I think you should go back there."

"Maybe tonight's the night there'll be something to make me shudder," Jamilla decided.

Back to the mansion she went; in through the gates at sunset. She found herself another candle. She went into the living room. She lit the fire. The clock struck nine. It struck ten. It struck eleven. It started chiming midnight. With the last chime of midnight, she heard a slow, soft voice. The voice was calling from up the chimney.

"I'm coming down," it said.

Jamilla was going to look up and see who the voice belonged to. She didn't have time. A leg came tumbling. She had to rescue it. She had to get it out of the fire.

The voice called again. It was slow and soft still.

"I'm coming down," it said.

Another leg fell. The voice called again.

"I'm coming down."

There was an arm.

"I'm coming down."

Another arm.

Jamilla was busy!

"I'm coming down."

The trunk of a man's body came *thunking*. The trunk was heavy. Jamilla checked the body parts out carefully. She went to the chimney.

"We need a head," she called.

A head came too, then. Jamilla arranged the head and the trunk, the arms and the legs, so they were in all the right places. She put them together. The man they belonged to sat up.

"Would you like a drink of water?" Jamilla asked him.

"I would," he answered.

Jamilla brought the water in a glass. The man drank the water. He thanked her. He walked off through the wall. Jamilla settled herself back in the rocking chair.

"I thought your mansion was where I was going to find out how to shudder," she said to the mansion's owner when she saw him in the morning.

"I'm sorry if it failed you," the mansion's owner said. "Still, I'm a man of my word. You stayed there three whole nights. The spell must be broken. I'll give you your reward."

Jamilla took the money. She thanked him.

"It's no good, is it?" she said to herself. "I can't learn to shudder. I just can't."

Then she thought how the money the mansion's owner had given her might be useful to her mother.

"I'll go home to her," she decided. "I'll stop going farther and farther, on and on."

She'd traveled a long distance by then. She'd walked all the way. She had to walk home as well. The journey took her a long, long while. When she came to where she could see her village, she got worried.

What if my mother has grown sick in all this time I've been away from her? she thought.

When she could see her own house, she started running.

What if something terrible has happened? What if my mother has died?

By the time she reached the door, she was shaking and shuddering all over.

"Mother! Oh, Mother!" she cried.

Her mother was there. She was as right as rain, but Jamilla started crying. "I was so afraid for you," she said.

"There's nothing the sight of you can't cure," her mother insisted.

"But if you should be lost to me. . . ."

"I'm not though, am I?"

Jamilla was shuddering worse than ever. She was shuddering so much her mother had to give her a hug and wrap her in a blanket and make her a cup of tea.

When Jamilla was better at last, the two of them sat together at the table talking over everything that had happened since they'd parted.

"I went all that way. I never shuddered until I got back to my own doorstep," Jamilla burst out.

"I expect there's a lesson in that," her mother told her.

"Most likely there is," Jamilla answered. "I won't think about that though, until the morning."

"We'll have our supper then," her mother said.

What's that at the door?

It's a story. I'm surprised you can't tell by yourself.

When it's putting its bags by the bedpost,

When it's laying its socks on the shelf.

I don't think we'll find one that's better,

Or one we'll be gladder to meet.

Not now, when the wind's all a-blowing,

And shaking the world at our feet.

FIVE

JACK GETS HIS FIRE

You can guess when this happened. It happened once upon a time.

That time now it wasn't my time or your time. It wasn't the time when the moon was made of good green cheese, either. It was the time when there were these three brothers and two of them were really smart, but one of them wasn't – and his name was Jack.

They lived together, all of them, in a town on the prairies. One fall they decided they'd go hunting. Ducks and geese are what they were hunting for. The best time for that's early in the morning, so they decided they'd camp out the night before, to be ready.

They chose themselves a good place. They set up their tent. They collected some sticks to make a fire. They'd have started to cook their supper, only they realized they'd left their matches on the table at home. They could see a farmhouse not so very far off in the distance.

"I reckon the farmer will have some matches he could give us," the oldest brother said.

He started toward the farmhouse as fast as he could run. The farmer was in the yard. He was seeing to his pigs.

"I'm in need of some matches to light a fire, so my brothers and I can cook our supper," the oldest brother said.

"I'll give you your matches if you'll sing me a song," the farmer replied.

The oldest brother didn't know any songs. He argued a bit, but he could see he wasn't getting anywhere. He had to go back empty-handed. His brothers weren't very happy about it.

"Let me try. I'm sure I can get some matches," the second brother declared.

He went off running as well. The farmer was on the back porch by that time; he was taking his boots off. His work was finished.

"I'm in need of some matches to light a fire, so my brothers and I can cook our supper," the second brother announced.

"I heard about that," the farmer said. "I'll be happy to give you your matches if you'll do me a dance."

"I don't know any dances."

"That's it then, isn't it?" said the farmer.

It was, too. The second brother had to come back to the camp empty-handed just like the first.

"I guess it's up to me," Jack said.

Not that he was in that much of a hurry. He set off at kind of a saunter. The farmer was in his kitchen. He was sitting in his rocking chair by the stove.

"Is there no end to you fellows?" he ranted.

"I'm the youngest; I'm the last," Jack said.

"Youngest or not, I suppose you're wanting matches?"

"It's so we can cook our supper."

"Supper or not, I believe one good turn deserves another."

"So my brothers have told me."

"Did the oldest say I asked him for a song?"

"He did, but I'm not much of a singer."

"Did the second say I asked him for a dance?"

"He did, but I don't dance, either."

"So why are you bothering me?"

"I thought maybe you'd like a story."

"Oh!" said the farmer, "A story! Well, maybe I would."

He pulled the rocking chair in closer. He put his feet up on a stool.

"Here's how it is," Jack told him. "This story I have – it's a good one. But it won't bear arguing with. If you should argue with it – at any point – I'll consider my part of the deal's over. I'll up and take the matches, whether you want to give them to me or not."

The farmer lit his pipe.

"Are you ready?" Jack asked him.

"I am," the farmer replied.

"Here's the way of it then," said Jack. "When I was younger still, I used to live north of here. I used to live in the woods. I had a horse. I used it for hauling logs. So on this one day, I was taking it to work with me."

"It's what I'd expect," the farmer said.

"Maybe you would," said Jack. "But here's what happened. I had my ax. I'd fixed it behind me, to my belt."

"It's what I'd expect."

"The horse got into trotting. The ax started bumping and banging all about. The ax bumped so hard it thunked the horse's rear end off. The tail end went one way. The head end went another. The head end was where I was riding. I kept on going."

"It's what I'd expect."

"Are you ready for more then?"

"Of course, I am."

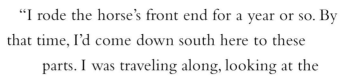

"I rode the horse's front end for a year or so. By that time, I'd come down south here to these parts. I was traveling along, looking at the scenery. I saw my horse's rear end in a field. I recognized that rear end from the markings."

"It's what I'd expect."

"Are you ready for more then?"

"Of course, I am."

"I wanted the two parts together. I got myself some thread. I stitched the front end and the rear end back the way they were supposed to be. I went off as right as rain. I wasn't very happy, though. The prairies were strange to me. I was pining for a glimpse of a tree. All of a sudden, I came upon one. It was the tallest tree I'd ever seen. I couldn't help myself. I thought a tree like that should be climbed."

"It's what I'd expect."

"Are you ready for more then?"

"Of course, I am."

"I got to the top of the tree. I found out I was in a whole new world. The thing that struck me was that flies were worth a stack of money; cattle weren't worth very much. I reckoned I'd come back down and collect myself some flies."

"It's what I'd expect."

"Are you ready for more then?"

"Of course, I am."

"I found the flies in a barn."

"It's what I'd expect."

"I put the flies in a sack. I carried the sack up. I sold the flies and I bought some cattle. I bought a whole great herd. I thought I'd made my fortune. I've never been so excited. The trouble was, by the time I got to where the top of the tree should have been, it wasn't there any more. Someone had chopped right through the trunk. I wanted to go home."

"It's what I'd expect."

"Are you ready for more then?"

"Of course, I am."

"I had to think about it. But I was desperate. I killed my cattle, right there on the spot. I used their hides to make a strap. The strap worked fine. I was sliding down it nicely. Only it wasn't long enough. When I got to the end of it I was still up in the air. I'd be there to this day, if a woman hadn't come out of her house and started husking corn. She was trying to throw the husks on a pile, but the wind was too strong for her. The wind kept carrying the husks up there to me. I reached out and I grabbed as many as I could manage. I used the husks to make a rope. I'd have been safe and sound in minutes, only the wind was blowing even harder."

"It's what I'd expect."

"Are you ready for more then?"

"Of course, I am."

"The rope was swinging and swaying. With all the swaying it broke. Down I came. There was a swamp beneath me – a slough. I fell right into it. I was up to my neck in water. I wasn't the only one in the swamp. A duck was there as well."

"It's what I'd expect."

"The duck was searching for a place to build her nest. She chose my hair. She laid her eggs, even. The eggs were just about to be hatching. A coyote saw the nest and he swam out. He scared the duck off; he swallowed the eggs down. The coyote was my chance. I grabbed his tail. I hollered to scare him. He was so frightened, he took off. Lucky he did. He pulled me out. I'm telling you, I looked dreadful."

"It's what I'd expect."

"I had swamp weeds round my ears. I had mud all over me. My clothes were making puddles. What was I to do, though? I walked and walked till I got to a road. I was going along the road when I saw this other fellow coming toward me. He was worse off than I was. He looked like his horse had bucked him in the muck heap and rolled on top of him. He smelled like you can't imagine."

"It's what I'd expect."

"I'm not so sure about that. Seeing as how, when I look at you, I know that you were him."

The farmer slammed down his pipe. He banged on the table.

"It couldn't have been me," he burst out.

Jack said nothing. The farmer jumped up. His face went red. His eyes started bulging.

"I'd die before I'd be seen in such a state," he thundered.

"Maybe you would and maybe you wouldn't," said Jack. "Either way, you're arguing with my story. Either way, I get my matches so my brothers and I can light our fire."

Jack took the matches; he was gone. His brothers were pleased to see him, that's for certain. The three of them got on with their cooking. They had a good supper and they had good hunting in the morning. Maybe if the farmer had been better to them, they might have given him a duck or two. As it was, they didn't have to bother. They just went home.

What's that at the door?

It's a story! It isn't a bull or a cow!
It's traveled a long way to see us.
It's mopping its sweaty, hot brow.

It just might be sent by a fairy.
It just might have come from the sea.
It just might be bringing some magic.
Some magic for you and for me.

JANE SAVES THE DAY

This story's about the meanest miser there's ever been in all the country's history. I hardly need to tell you when it happened. It happened once upon a time – the time that wasn't my time or your time, but has to have been his time, somewhere back there in the dim and distant past.

The miser lived in a beautiful place by a wide and flowing river with ships sailing on it. He was called the Master, because he owned everything as far as anyone could go. He had more money than he knew what to do with, but all he ever thought about was how to get more.

The Master had a lot of servants. One of those servants was called Jane. Jane had a lowly job in the kitchen. She had to wash pile upon pile of dishes; she had to scrub floors on her hands and knees; she had to carry out the cinders. Still, she was always smiling. The only thing she ever grumbled about was her hair. It was so curly it kept springing out from under her servant's cap. The cook was always yelling at her to pin her hair back up.

The Master didn't know about Jane. The Master didn't know about any of his servants. Not really. All he cared about was getting more work out of them. A day came when he called them together in the yard so he could explain to them how they were going to have to toil away for even longer hours, and get even less for themselves in wages.

Jane was there, of course. She had to be.

"I want servants who are tireless," the Master announced.

There was a great big clap of thunder. An enormous Genie appeared out of a cloud. The Genie stood before the Master, bowing.

"I am tireless and I am yours to command," the Genie said.

The Master looked like he might dance with joy. The Genie bowed lower.

"I will do anything you wish, but there is one thing you must know about me. I have to be kept working. If I am left idle – even for a moment – I shall start to devour you from head to foot."

The Master was so busy thinking of all he could get done, he hardly listened to the last part. The servants were so worried about how the Genie was going to take their jobs away, they weren't listening properly, either. Jane paid attention.

I'll remember that, she thought.

"You can start by building me a new barn," the Master told the Genie.

The Genie went to work. The servants watched in amazement. The Genie could hardly be seen he was moving so quickly. In less than an hour, the barn was finished. The Master looked even happier. He looked happier than he'd ever done in his whole life.

"There's a new parcel of land I want cleared," he told the Genie. "I'll ride with you in my carriage to show you where it is."

The Genie set off, two fields at a stride. The Master could hardly keep up to him.

"That Genie will be the end of us," the servants said.

"I wouldn't be too sure," said Jane.

At evening, the Master came back. The Genie had cleared the new parcel of land. He'd also repaired all the fences and widened all the ditches. The Master set him to building another wing onto the house.

By morning, the Genie had the new wing ready. The Master sent him out to dig a lake. The job would have taken the servants months. The Genie had it done by lunchtime. The servants were even more worried. They started trying to figure out how the Genie might be got rid of.

"Better to spend your time imagining what it would be like to have the Genie work for us," said Jane.

Now that she'd put the idea into their heads, the servants couldn't stop themselves imagining. After all, the houses the Master gave them to live in were all so tumbledown.

"I'd have the Genie fix my roof so it didn't leak!" said the head gardener.

"I'd have the Genie mend my walls so they weren't falling into pieces," said the butler.

"I'd have the Genie repair the holes in my floors and set my doors back on their hinges," said the cook.

The Genie went on following the Master's instructions. He rounded up the sheep. He sheared them. He took the wool to the mill. He got the machines at the mill running. He carded the wool. He spun it and wove it.

He straightened the stream so it would flow faster. He trimmed the hedges in the gardens. He mowed the wide, green lawns. He planted saplings for a new forest. He washed the Master's windows. He washed his whole house.

That was all finished by the end of the second day. The servants, whose jobs the Genie was doing, were getting hungry. They weren't being paid.

"You keep imagining anyway," Jane told them. "You keep on thinking what that Genie might do for you."

The Master gave his orders. The Genie worked through the second night. He cleaned the cowsheds and built a couple of extra ones for good measure. He sluiced down the pig sties. He polished the horses' coats. He plowed the fields of summer fallow. He cleaned the paths. He weeded the vegetables. He built two new docks. He unloaded a boat that had brought supplies.

In the morning, the servants noticed the Master wasn't looking so happy. There were dark circles under his eyes as if he hadn't slept a wink.

"You remember what's going to happen to the Master if the Genie isn't kept working?" Jane asked them.

All of a sudden, the servants did. When the orchard man came hurrying to tell them the Genie was picking apples and pears that were still green, it occurred to them maybe the Master was running out of ideas.

The Genie was getting bigger too. He was working faster and faster. The Master was looking more and more terrified. By evening, while the Genie was scything a field that didn't need scything because the hay hadn't grown above an inch or so, the Master was trembling. The Master was tearing out his hair. The Master was pacing backward and forward, muttering. The servants had never seen anything like it.

"Now's our chance," Jane said.

The servants were still nervous. They decided the head gardener should go first.

"Master, Master, my roof is leaking," the head gardener pleaded.

To the servants' surprise, the Master almost kissed him. The servants sent the butler at a run.

"Master, Master, my walls are falling over," the butler cried out.

The Master almost gave him a hug. The cook couldn't see any further reason for delaying.

"Master, Master, my floor has holes! My doors are off their hinges," she almost shouted.

The Master looked as if he might kneel down at her feet. Before the night was out, the Genie had made every single one of the servants' homes more comfortable than they could have dreamed.

The shepherd asked for a school. The Master had the Genie build it. The gardener's boy wanted everyone's wood chopped for the winter. The Master had the Genie do that. Someone else thought of how the chimneys needed sweeping; how the potholes should be filled in on the paths. The chambermaid decided she'd like a park with a fountain and shade trees to walk amongst on summer evenings. The forester's son wanted a swimming hole. The coachman thought they could all of them do with their houses that were now so comfortable, made a little bigger, so they'd have more room.

The best of it was that every time the servants went to the Master, he begged them to think of more and more and MORE. He thanked them for their efforts. He wept tears of gratitude. He praised people. The servants thought they'd died and gone to heaven. No one could ever remember the Master praising anyone. Praising people wasn't what the Master did.

Still, after two more days, the servants were exhausted. The hammering and banging and changing things was keeping them awake at night as well. Try as they might, they couldn't think of anything else they wanted.

The Genie wasn't as big as a house, or even two houses. The Genie was as big as a village. He looked like he wouldn't stop with the Master. He'd devour everyone and everything in sight.

The Master wasn't the only one quaking in fear and horror. The servants were as well.

"You're sure you've got everything you wanted?" Jane asked them.

"We've got more than we wanted," the servants replied.

"My turn," Jane said.

She went to the Master while he had the Genie trying to shear the sheep again.

"Would you like to see the Genie gone?" she asked.

"I'd give anything to see the Genie gone," the Master answered.

"I can tell you how to do it," Jane said. "But you'll have to promise you'll go on treating us the way you should do."

"I promise! I promise!" the Master burst out.

"There won't be any forgetting?"

"There won't! There won't!"

Jane sat herself down. Jane made herself comfortable. Jane took off her servant's cap. She pulled one of the hairs from off the top of her head.

"My curls keep getting me into trouble," she told the Master. "I've always thought if I could get just one hair straightened I'd be better off. I've tried to do it myself, but I can't seem to manage it."

"The Genie will do it in an instant."

"You must tell him not to harm it."

"I'll be devoured for certain."

"It's worth a try," said Jane.

The Genie was striding back. He was carrying the little bit of wool he'd managed to gather. The sky was darkening with his approach. The Master was desperate. One instant to go on living seemed better than no instants. The Master took Jane's hair and held it out.

"You're to straighten this hair and you're not to harm it," the Master murmured.

The Genie looked at the Master as if he was considering what kind of a meal he'd make. The Genie took the hair between his two great hands. The Genie licked his lips.

He pulled on the hair. He straightened it, but only for an instant. As soon as he let one end go, the curls came back. The Genie rubbed the hair between his fingers. The Genie started frowning. The Genie rubbed the hair against his vest.

He put the hair on the ground. He stood on it. He stamped it. He brought a bucket. He filled the bucket with water. He plunged the hair in. The curls were still there. The Genie stretched the hair between his teeth.

For two whole days the Genie worked at the hair and worked at it. He ran over it with cart wheels. He crushed it between bricks. He tied one end to the clothesline and weighted the other. He roared at the hair, he spat on it. He shook it in the wind.

All the while he was getting angrier and angrier. Smoke was coming out of his nostrils almost, flames from out of his ears. Finally, the Genie took off. He had the hair with him. He was howling. The hair wasn't any straighter than it had been in the beginning. Most likely he's howling and working at it still.

One thing's for certain; the Genie didn't come back. The Master waited a week or so, in case. When the week was up, he

organized a great feast. The feast was for the servants so they could celebrate. After that, the Master didn't forget his promise about treating them better. He became kindness itself to them. Everyone was much, much happier than they'd been before.

As for Jane, the cook said she didn't have to wear her servant's cap again. Not ever. She wouldn't have had to anyway, because the Master gave her a whole lot of money to live on to thank her for her help. First she went on a journey down the river; then she went up it; then she came back.

The money the Master provided meant she only had to work when she wanted. That's what she did then. She only did the kind of work she wanted to, as well. Mostly she spent her time helping people with their troubles. It didn't seem to matter what problem anyone brought her. She always had some sort of an answer. Folks said she could have dealt with a hundred Genies if she'd had to. Still, they were glad enough to find that there wasn't even one more Genie that appeared.

A NOTE ON SOURCES

JESPER AND THE JACKRABBITS. This is from a Scandinavian tale which I found in *The Violet Fairy Book* among the stories collected and edited by Andrew Lang (New York: Dover Publications, 1967). Lang's version is entitled, "Jesper Who Herded the Hares."

JACINTHE WINS WORDS. From *Speak Bird, Speak Again. Palestinian Arab Folktales* by Ibrahim Muhawi and Sharif Kanaana (Los Angeles: University of California Press, 1989). In that book, the story is called, "The Rich Man and the Poor Man" although it is still very clearly about two sisters.

A CAT AND MOUSE TALE. From a story collected by Helen Creighton in Canada, as part of her book *A Folk Tale Journey Through the Maritimes* (Wreck Cove: Breton Books, 1993). That version is called, "The Old Cat Spinning in the Oven."

JAMILLA FINDS FEAR. This story has a large number of antecedents. It was set down by the Brothers Grimm as "The Story of the Youth Who Went Forth to Learn What Fear Was" and is also found adapted from a Turkish version in Andrew Lang's *The Olive Fairy Book* (New York: Dover Publications, 1967). I have added elements from "Down Come a Leg," collected in Virginia by Richard Chase. I have never found the story with a girl as the central character, however.

JACK GETS HIS FIRE. From "Jack and the Beekeeper" as collected by Alan Garner for his book *A Bag of Moonshine* (London: William Collins & Sons, 1986).

JANE SAVES THE DAY. From a Tamil tale entitled, "A Hair's-Breadth Escape" published in *Folktales from India: A Selection of Oral Tales from Twenty-two Languages*, selected and edited by A.K. Ramanujan as part of *The Pantheon Fairy Tale and Folklore Library* (New York: Pantheon Books, 1991).